Hard to Get Lucky

(Book Two of the Hard to Get Series)

by Jenny Gardiner

Chapter One

Fifteen years earlier

FIFTH grader Alyssa Heyward had been looking forward to Caitlyn Colby's birthday sleepover party for weeks. It was the first party she'd been invited to since her family moved to town. She and Caitlyn had hit it off quite readily, so this would be the perfect chance to hang out with other kids from Roland Clark Elementary School. In most cases, she only saw them while they sat at their assigned desks during the school day. And there would be boys for the birthday party part of the evening—Alyssa's first co-ed party! She was nervous but excited.

On the day of the event, she'd pulled her long, blond hair into a French braid—with help from her mom—and even snuck into her mom's makeup and applied a discreet amount of eye shadow to highlight her pale green eyes. She put on her favorite knit sundress with the rainbows on it over a pair of black capri leggings. She knew she'd fit right in.

At the party, things went great early on: all the kids swam in Caitlyn's backyard pool, and Caitlyn's dad grilled the best hot dogs and hamburgers. The birthday cake was Alyssa's favorite: yellow cake with buttercream frosting. All good. But then the kids migrated to Caitlyn's basement and someone decided they all had to play spin the bottle.

Hard to Get Lucky

Alyssa wasn't all that enlightened when it came to boys and had never kissed one. There were some cute boys in her classes, and there were some who grossed her out. Like that boy Josh Trumbull, who was super gross and whose claim to dubious fame was that he'd eaten a fly in the cafeteria, although perhaps even worse, he loved to burp and fart like he was some sort of pig in a farmyard. She was dismayed to see him at the party, and of course he behaved horribly. After jamming a hot dog down his throat in record time, he mustered up the loudest, most disgusting burp imaginable, like some totally vomitrocious percussion instrument. He wouldn't be so awful if he wasn't so crass. He could almost be cute, with his kind brown eyes, and she kind of liked when boys had dark wavy hair. But yuck—there was no way she'd even *stand* near Josh Trumbull, even if someone paid her a million dollars.

At first, when the twenty or so kids descended into the basement, they all played video games in the room where the girls had already set up their sleeping bags. Alyssa watched from the corner of her eye to be sure stinky Josh, who kids called The Mad Tooter, didn't settle down near her bag. The last thing she wanted was him smelling up her comfy pink sleeping bag with the kitties and puppies on it.

Then some tall boy named Luis stood up and let out a whistle to get everyone's attention as he pulled out a bottle of Coke he'd tucked into the waistband of his jeans.

"Gather round," he said, motioning to the crowd. "Everyone get in a big circle here. Now we're gonna have some real fun."

Oh God, what is he talking about? Alyssa wished she could slip upstairs and grab another slice of that delicious cake, or maybe even help Mrs. Colby with the dishes. She feared the telltale bottle could only be the harbinger of bad things to come.

He plunked the bottle down in the center of the group of kids who were tittering and giggling and whispering.

"All right, people," he said over the noise of excited tweens. How someone his age could have such a command of the group mystified Alyssa. She was perfectly happy to blend into the room and avoid being noticed. "I'm gonna get this party started with the first spin of the bottle. If the bottle lands pointing at a boy, I get to spin again. But if it lands pointing to a girl, then we go there." He aimed his thumb over his shoulder, pointing toward the storage room where Alyssa knew Caitlyn's much older sister Samantha went to smoke cigarettes and drink beer with her friends. Caitlyn and Alyssa had caught them in there on more than one occasion when Alyssa slept over.

Alyssa's eyes widened. By "we go there" did he mean what she was afraid he meant? This was the dreaded game, the one all fifth graders had heard about, the one that instilled fear in the hearts of burgeoning tweens everywhere. You're forced by peer pressure to slip off alone into a small, enclosed space with someone you don't even know and press your lips together. Ugh. This terrified her.

Luis's bottle stopped, pointing toward a quiet girl named Ginny whose face turned bright red when she knew she was the first victim. She glanced around at her friends to see if they would grant her a respite, but instead, she encountered jeers and cheers.

Luis extended his hand and grabbed Ginny's and the next thing everybody knew, they were inside that storage room and everyone in the circle waited in near silence till they'd done the deed.

When they emerged, Luis licking his lips like a wolf after finishing off a delicious sheep, Alyssa didn't know what to make of things. Ginny was still blushing, only she had a slight grin, which was better than the flat-out tears Alyssa had half expected though still unnerving. Had Ginny actually *liked* it?

Round after round, girls and boys paired off for their slow walk to the storage room.

Then came Josh Trumbull's turn. To make sure his presence was known, he took a fat swig of his own bottle of soda and forced out a belch that practically vibrated throughout the room. He was disgusting. Standing in the center of the group, he bent down to spin the bottle, and—no lie—tooted out a blast of air from his backside that made Alyssa cringe. Pity the poor girl who would be stuck in there with him. She'd need a gas mask.

He gave the bottle a dramatic whirl with a strong flick of his wrist, and Alyssa stared as the bottle circled around again and again before slowing. She clasped her fingers together in prayer. "*Pleasepleaseplease, don't let it be me,*" repeated on an endless loop in her head.

The bottle seemed to enter into some time warp slo-mo as it crept to a dead stop at last, pointing right at Alyssa. The girls on either side of her even shifted away from her to ensure there was no confusion as to who the victim would be.

Alyssa's face fell. It felt as if the blood had drained from it. For a split second she wondered if she might faint dead away on the spot, which would be equally mortifying. Talk about a lose-lose proposition. Although maybe passing out would be the hall pass she needed to get out of this dirty deed. Josh Trumbull stood in front of her, performing dire pelvic thrusts in her direction, making her almost gag as he crooked his pointer finger at her, then curled it back toward him so she knew in no uncertain terms there was no choice but to suffer through this indignity.

Closing her eyes, she tried to invoke happy thoughts: beach trips with her family, swimming in the ocean with her dog Lupe, snuggling at bedtime with her kitten Muffin, an A on her history test. She stood up and her bare feet almost betrayed her by obliging Josh Trumbull's coaxing finger. As she followed a few paces behind him, she hoped everyone in the room realized she had no choice but to subjugate herself for the greater good of her contemporaries at Roland Clark Elementary School. There was no hope of a stay of execution. She gulped hard; this was the twenty-first-century version of walking the gangplank on a pirate ship on the Barbary Coast.

The light was on in the room when they entered it, giving Alyssa enough time to scour the horizon and see that her safest harbor was in the far left corner of the room, past the stacked boxes marked "Christmas Decorations," but then Josh Trumbull turned to face his audience of one as he dramatically pulled the cord belonging to the naked bulb above, extinguishing the light and bathing the room in darkness as he slammed the door for effect.

Alyssa wanted to cry. God, if she had to put her face close to his mouth, would it smell like dead flies? Probably not, because the other part of him that always stunk would overpower it. This was so unfair. Why couldn't it have been someone like Christian Masterson, who at least chewed gum 24/7 so he'd have fresh, minty breath? Or better yet, Rodrigo Lopez, who everyone knew would only share his kisses with the boys. She'd be totally safe and kiss-free in the dark with him.

As she stood stock-still, the lingering aroma of Samantha's noxious cigarette smoke and stale beer permeated the air. The silence in the room was agonizing. She surely wasn't going to say a peep. Besides, opening her mouth seemed a bad idea anyhow, what with his mouth lurking threateningly somewhere in close proximity.

"So, uh, you coming over anytime soon?" he said at last.

"No thank you," Alyssa said.

"'*No thank you*' as in you're not coming over here and you'd rather I come to you?"

She shook her head—not like he could see it. "No, thank you. I'm fine here in this corner all alone."

"You're not even going to give me a kiss?"

"No thank you." She sounded like a broken record.

"That's lame."

They stood there, barely conversing, with Alyssa only repeating her new, albeit polite, mantra.

"Fine, then. If you're gonna be that way about it."

Alyssa didn't know how someone could command bodily functions at a whim like this boy could, but sure enough he could, and he discharged the stinkiest, loudest emission of bodily gas she'd ever encountered in her short time on earth. Being brotherless, she was simply not used to this sort of ickiness.

"That's disgusting," she said, plugging her nose with her fingers.

"Takes one to know one," he said with a dopey laugh. Which didn't even make sense, but whatever.

Enough arduous time had passed that kids started pounding on the door, so Josh Trumbull opened it wide, the brightness near blinding after she'd been in complete darkness for several minutes.

Everyone clamored to find out how it went.

"Well," he said, standing in the middle of the circle as Alyssa slunk back to her spot and sat down. "We never got around to kissing because she let out a huge fart and stunk up the whole room."

"Ewww," all the girls shouted.

"Cool," said one guy. Another guy gave her a thumbs-up.

Everyone turned to look at Alyssa, who hung her head, mortified.

The rest of the night was a bit of a blur. Alyssa did her best to blend in with the background. People kept coming up to her and asking if she'd really farted in there, and she was so upset and disgusted she could barely speak. In the months to follow, Alyssa's classmates would tease her mercilessly for what happened—or didn't happen—that night. It defined the remaining time of elementary school for her, and not in a good way.

That night was the last time she ever had anything to do with Josh Trumbull for the rest of her academic career, for which she couldn't have been more thrilled. If she never saw him again in her whole life, it would be fine by her.

Chapter Two

ALYSSA was finishing breakfast when the doorbell rang. Finally, the contractor must have arrived to start the long-awaited addition to her house.

She'd been lucky and had unexpected success in her writing career when her first novel hit it big—something most writers hope their whole lives for. That meant some welcome financial security after years of toiling in obscurity and postponing bills whenever possible to keep the lights on. It also meant she could quit her job to write full-time. And it meant the tiny fixer-upper she'd purchased on the cheap in the Northern Virginia suburbs was finally going to morph into the cozy home she'd envisioned. Aside from an overhaul of her dingy kitchen, she was adding on a whole new two-story section to the house—which would mean a guest bedroom for visitors—plus a gorgeous black-bottom swimming pool out back and a dedicated office where she could focus while writing, rather than forever hunkering down over the dining room table as she'd done for years.

The housing boom meant she'd lost three general contractors to bigger jobs right before the scheduled construction. The last one was a kind man, though, who'd felt bad enough about it to send someone reliable in his stead. And that someone was waiting for Alyssa to open the door.

She felt an inexplicable need to primp for a second

before so doing, stupidly thinking if she looked decent enough and not like, say, a bleary-eyed, bed-headed, coffee-breathed writer who'd stayed up till almost dawn to work on her latest novel, the guy would stick around and actually do the work. She was so tired of waiting.

She ran her fingers through her hair and slid her glasses up on her head as she pulled the door open.

"Hi!" she blurted out before having a chance to unblurt it. Because standing before her could only be none other than Josh "The Mad Tooter" Trumbull—unmistakable in his appearance despite the passage of some fifteen years. She could instantly feel her face fall, the broad beam of a smile transforming into a grimace that spoke volumes.

No greater humiliation than one foisted upon you in childhood could linger quite so bitterly. At least that's what Alyssa told herself as she ground her molars together with such intensity that she thought she'd crack a filling. The shame cast upon her at the ripe age of ten had hung around far more intensely than she would have imagined. Because the mere sight of that dirty ratfink Josh Trumbull ricocheted her right back to that embarrassing night in Caitlyn Colby's basement.

Pretending not to know who he was, she squinted curiously, as if unfamiliar with him. Though he had to know who she was because her former contractor must have given him her name.

"Alyssa!" He reached out for a hug, which of all the damned things wasn't going to happen in this lifetime. "So great to see you after all these years!"

A silence fell over them as he stood at the threshold to her home—good Lord, the threshold to her very *life*. He'd be in her home every damned day until he finished this huge project while she tried to write and function and not simmer

9

in rage.

This is what it had come to? Finally fixing up her grungy, 1950s-era Northern Virginia red brick rambler—the only house she could afford with eye-popping DC-area prices when she bought it—meant welcoming her lifelong nemesis into said home and pretending she was happy about it?

She closed her eyes and mentally counted to ten. Opening them, she fixed the scowl so that her mouth was a tight line across her face. She reached out her hand to shake his, with no plans whatsoever to touch him even more with that hug he was attempting to foist on her.

"Josh? Josh 'The Mad Tooter' Trumbull? Well, who'd have thought I'd ever be seeing you again."

Worse still, who'd have thought she'd have to practically share her life with him for the next several months? At least this time, no one would expect her to kiss him. If she had her way, she'd not even have to speak to him. Time would tell.

Chapter Three

FROM the day that cute little Alyssa Heyward showed up at Roland Clark Elementary School with her long, blond braid and those green eyes with such long lashes—was it in fifth grade?—Josh Trumbull had always harbored a crush on the girl. Back then, he wasn't exactly a pro with the ladies. In retrospect, he was pretty stupid, if he had to admit it. He thought drawing the attention of a cute girl was all it took, so he did some stupid things to make sure they noticed him.

Once he ate a fly in the cafeteria—which wasn't as nasty as it could have been—likely because he swallowed it whole rather than chewing on it. He popped a tiny tree frog in his mouth at a year-end class party then spat it out onto Margaret Sampson's lap, which he thought was freaking hilarious. Oddly she wasn't charmed by that one.

In general, he'd loved to fart in front of people. After all, what boy didn't? Yet he seemed to relish it more than most, letting one rip when least expected. And he soaked up the crowd response whenever he did. Sure, it grossed them out a bit, but it got him noticed, and that felt great. It might have taken him a tiny bit of therapy years later to realize that his need to be noticed was rooted in his parents' inattention. Too busy fighting with each other, his folks paid him no mind. He probably could've set the house on fire and they'd never have heard the roar of the ensuing fire above their shouting. By the time his parents split up at the end of elementary school, he was a permanent afterthought from there on out. His mom was too busy holding down two jobs. His dad, who was career military, shipped off to Japan or Korea or something like that and disappeared from his life.

He'd had no idea how to get Alyssa to notice him. Unskilled at the fine art of conversation, the only tool in his social cues tool belt was being a jackass. Though he'd at last dealt with his issues and motives with a great therapist as an adult, he hadn't focused at all on how his actions affected others. Quite honestly, he couldn't imagine that the behavior of a dopey boy would have affected anyone in any way, anyhow!

Although back in the day, he was proud of how he'd put that Alyssa in her place at Caitlyn Colby's birthday party when she shunned him. He'd done nothing to her, ever, and there they were in that dark room on the night of the spin the bottle game and she treated him like a pariah. His one chance alone with her where he could wow her with his personality, and she was the high-and-mighty princess casting him aside for no good reason. Whatever stick was up her ass was her problem, not his. Even though for the rest of the time they were in school together, his heart still skipped a tiny beat each time he saw her after that, longing for her to realize that he was worthy of her attention.

When his buddy Mac passed this contracting job on to him, he hadn't known the name of the client yet. And when he did find out who it was, he was more than a bit curious about her. He'd spent a lot of years angry at her, resentful for her being one more human who'd shunned him. Come to think of it, she'd rejected him one more time in middle school, when rumors of his intentions to ask her to the homecoming dance yielded a firm warning from Caitlyn to not dare do that. Despite all this, he was still a little intrigued.

Had she become a nicer person as an adult? He'd heard she was a successful author who'd won some big-deal awards and sold lots of books. He wasn't much of a reader and hadn't rushed out to buy any of hers.

Besides, he was still a bit mentally dug in against her. Maybe not quite the "fuck you, Alyssa Heyward" dug in, but still, he wasn't necessarily in the mood to make nice. Which is why he surprised himself by reaching out to hug her when she opened the door. *What the hell, Joshy-boy? You're not supposed to hug your enemy.* Nope. Not even if she looked pretty damned hot in a pair of running shorts and a flimsy, sleeveless jogging shirt that absorbed sweat but clung to her enough to reveal her perfectly shaped breasts. Not that he hadn't noticed them back in middle school before she and Josh went their separate ways to different high schools a few years later. She was always a pretty, perfect princess without a blemish on her face and the icy blond hair, translucent green eyes, and rockin' body that only got better with age.

It didn't escape him that she refused his hug, either. He'd give her the benefit of the doubt, what with the shock factor and all.

"Yeah, right, crazy that we're being reunited this way," Josh said. "I mean, what are the chances?"

He wanted to smack himself with that dopey comment. *What are the chances?* Geez. She still left him tongue-tied.

"Yeeeaaahhh," she said, drawing out the word into about five syllables as if she couldn't think of anything more useful or compelling to say. She crossed her arms over her lovely breasts, which displeased him even more, what with obscuring his view, not to mention exhibiting hostility. "What are the chances?"

He stood there in the doorway, wondering if she was going to invite him in. He'd taken a look at the outside of the place before ringing the bell. It looked like it had good bones. He loved taking a crotchety old home and turning it into a more time-relevant showplace—or at least a far more livable space for the twenty-first century.

He wiped his hands on the sides of his jeans, then nodded. "Looks like you've got quite the project here."

She pressed her fingertips to her forehead as if staving off a headache, then smiled that tepid smile that said she'd rather be waiting for the dentist to drill out all her teeth than stand here talking to him. He wasn't stupid. He got it: she still hated him.

"Oh. Yeah. That." She turned to look inside the house and shook her head. "Ah, yes. Sorry about that. The project." She motioned with her hand. It looked like she was swatting at a fly rather than beckoning him into her private sanctuary. "Come on in and I'll give you the tour."

He stepped into the foyer and she stopped, staring at his muddy work boots. Taking the hint, he removed them before entering the main part of the house. She'd better not expect that for the next few months, 'cause he'd be coming and going a ton and didn't have time for lacing and unlacing his boots. Usually his clients understood it was part of the package. No doubt it bothered him more, simply because she was making it clear that she thought he had cooties. Well, if she was going to treat him like an untouchable, fine. He was here to do a job, not make friends. It was a shame to see that ole Alyssa Heyward was nothing more than a grown-up version of the snob she was when she was ten. Whatever.

Chapter Four

AS Alyssa led Josh through the house, pointing out details about what she wanted and which things took priority, part of her wanted to gawk at the man she'd hated for so long, which surprised her. 'Cause, well, he was a pretty damned good-looking man, all beefy and strong, and he still had that brown wavy hair. Only now, she kept thinking it might be nice to run her fingers through it. Alyssa had a thing for smiling eyes and his smiling brown eyes were no exception. But no, touching his hair could not possibly be nice. Although it might be. Except this was Josh Trumbull. Ugh.

At one point, she found herself standing behind him while he surveyed the backyard. His jeans hugged his ass so perfectly that... well, he might have been disgusting, but she'd be a liar if she didn't admit he was pretty hot. She closed her eyes against the thoughts she was entertaining. Thoughts that involved her taking one of those running leaps into his arms and wrapping her sweaty legs around his waist and feeling the hard length of him pressed up against her and...

No. Just no. She shook her head out of her reverie. There would be no grinding with Josh Trumbull. As if on cue, a fly whizzed by her head, reminding her in no uncertain terms that this guy was an unwelcome blast from the past. After finishing this project, he'd move way back on the dusty shelves of her memory, never to be visited again.

"So, if it's all the same to you, I need to get back to work now. I'll leave you to it."

"Cool," Josh said, holding the back door for her to go inside. "Since Danny and I have talked extensively, and he already had everything lined up and ready to get started, give me a couple of days and I'll plan on starting first thing Monday morning."

Alyssa was so conflicted. All she wanted was a finished addition on her house. But ugh, she did not look forward to having Josh Trumbull in her life nonstop for the next several months. She hated to admit it, but everyone has their price. And hers, it seemed, came down to tolerating the last man she ever wanted in her life, completely in her life. Crap.

Josh was pretty excited about this unexpected renovation job. Mostly because he loved sinking his teeth into a new project, and he couldn't wait to see the final product. He thought this one would be awesome when done, and he'd have an opportunity to use his woodworking skills as well, which always made him happiest.

He was good at what he did and always happy to please his customers. And he'd love to please *this* particular customer, as she seemed hard to please—at least when it came to him. Come to think of it, he'd love to give pleasure to this particular customer because every time he was around her, he had to tamp down the damned boner that kept threatening to give him away. Especially the morning when she opened the door in a cute little pajama outfit that consisted of tiny, thin cotton shorts that barely hugged her ass and a tank top revealing the unmistakable outline of her nipples. He'd damned near hyperventilated. But aside from looking sexy as hell, she was still disinterested in him, which made him crazy. How could someone be so stubborn about something that happened a damned lifetime ago? Besides, on balance, she probably humiliated him in public more than he did her. At least he'd put himself out there with her. But he wouldn't do that now. If she wanted to stonewall him, so be it. He'd sneak peeks at her hot tits and ass when he could and go home and jack off, fantasizing about how she'd look naked.

After working at Alyssa's place for about two weeks, he'd accepted that engaging in conversation with her was a challenge. He always did the right things: He knocked before entering, even though he didn't have to. He removed his damned boots each time he came in, even if it was to walk from the front hall to the back of the house, only to have to put them back on again. He checked if he was being too loud when he was knocking down some drywall.

At best, he elicited one- or two-word answers. She'd look up from her computer, practically grunt "yes" or "no," then avert her gaze back to the screen. At first it bothered him, but then he viewed it as a challenge. Maybe he'd get her to grow the hell up and act like a normal adult around him. It wasn't as if he'd sprouted horns and breathed fire since that time long ago when they'd known each other. She made him horny as hell, though he'd tried not to stoke that fire of temptation. Otherwise, he might accidentally reach over and pinch a nipple when she came back from a run wearing her short shorts and the flimsy spandex shirt someday. He clearly was on to something when he had a mad boyhood crush on her all those years ago. But now it wasn't a crush he was nursing, it was an all-out desire to figure out how to get her to come around, and eventually get her to come with his hard cock deep inside her. He always did like a challenge, and this would be one for the ages.

and benefits and job security."

"Lyssa, honey. Your book has sat on the *New York Times* best-seller list for over a year. As much as I'd like to indulge your financial pity party, I know for a fact that you can afford to spring for your own dinner."

Alyssa thrust out her bottom lip. "All right, fine. So I'm not in dire financial straits. I'm more in a funk and mentally catastrophizing in case I can't write this next book. And then what? I'm a washed-up has-been and can't ever get a publishing house to trust me again and all my income and speaking fees will dry up and—"

"Dude! Whooooa whoooa whooooa. Chill the hell out! Look, you know I'm always down with meeting my big sister for dinner. Hell, I might even decide to pay for you. And I know the perfect place to cheer you up. Meet you at Sumo in an hour. I'll call ahead and get our name on a list."

"You're the best little sister a girl could ask for. Plus, you know the best way to my happiness is through my stomach, especially with hibaachi."

"The good thing about going to a Japanese steak house is you don't even have to put on makeup!" Alyssa ran squealing up to her sister, arms outstretched, and pulled her into a big hug.

"Hell, I don't even bother with a bra."

Alyssa held her finger to her lips. "Shhh! You can't be talking about undergarments among a bunch of strangers waiting to sit at the same dinner table as you!"

Her sister swatted her hand away. "Are you crazy?

They're the very best people to discuss such things with," she said. "I love to talk about the most intimate things with folks I've never met and will never see again. Imagine if I bring up something really awful, like, say, yeast infections!"

"Oh my God, Katrina. I came here to be distracted, not disgusted!"

Kat elbowed her in the side. "You know I'm just ribbing you. I always knew how to push your buttons." She grinned and linked arms with Alyssa, leading the way. "Come on, they're waiting to seat us."

The hostess escorted them to a communal table—full of strangers, natch—with two empty chairs, and they sat.

"We'd like two of the jumbo hot sakes please, stat," Kat said before she even sat down.

"I will be asleep in my plate if I drink that much."

"Oh, please. I visited you in college. I know you've got the alcohol tolerance of Don Draper in Mad Men."

Alyssa smacked her arm. "So maybe I used a little bad judgment in my glory days."

"Don't tell me you're past your glory days, Lyss."

They opened their menus and perused their options.

"Honestly I don't even know why I bother looking." Alyssa sighed. "I always get the same damned thing."

"When variety can be the spice of life."

"Meh, I guess my theme now would be that uniformity is the spice of life." Alyssa frowned. "I'm not sure uniformity is the exact opposite of variety, but whatever."

The waitress returned with the sakes and prepared to take their orders, and Alyssa pointed to the chicken and shrimp combo.

Kat scruffed her hair. "Seriously, girl, you need to mix it up. You've become an old fuddy-duddy."

"Says the woman who used the term 'fuddy-duddy.'

What are you, my granny?"

"You've got a point. I don't know why I came up with that." She took a swig of her sake, fanning her mouth from the heat. "But anyhow, why don't you challenge yourself a bit. Step outside your comfort zone. Like do something you would never think to do to make yourself uncomfortable."

Alyssa sipped her sake, choking on it at the idea that crossed her mind suddenly. "Oh God, no. No way. No no no no no."

Kat's eyes grew wide. "Whatever it is, I can tell it's a great big yes. Come on, spill it."

The chef rolled his cart up to the table, greeted them all, and began to perform his chefly tricks, slicing and dicing and spinning and tossing. The diners at the table clapped appropriately when he flipped an egg into the concave top of his chef's toque.

"I can't even mention this to you, Katrina, because I know you'll try to make me do something that would be the worst thing I could ever imagine doing."

Kat threw back some more sake. "As if I had that power over you. Come on—spill it. What are you withholding?"

Alyssa pushed her plate closer to the scorching-hot stainless steel table so the chef could shovel her cooked food onto it. "I can't even begin to tell you how much joy this brings me." She speared a piece of shrimp and popped it into her mouth, rolling her eyes back. "Sublime."

"You are so good at dodging my probing questions. But I'm going to extract what I need from you. I've always managed to do that. You might as well give it up willingly, or I'll have to force tickle you."

Alyssa held up her hands. "No, please, not that. Fine, I'll confess." She held a finger up for a second then reached for her drink and took a big gulp. Thank goodness she had

Uber to get her home. "You know how I keep losing general contractors for my big home reno, right? The last one, Danny, was a sure bet. But then he got an offer he couldn't refuse for a much bigger project than mine, and I didn't want to be a jerk and insist that he honor his commitment. In turn, he told me he'd find a replacement—"

"Which was what he should do."

"Yeah, well, certainly not what the others did, so that was a nice gesture."

"Yay! So now what's the problem?"

"Sooo… the new guy showed up the other day and—"

"And he's superhot and you want to have one of those porn flick experiences where the hot dude with the bulge in his pants shows up to work on your plumbing and you're dressed in a skimpy outfit and the next thing you know you're in the hot tub straddling the guy?"

Alyssa shook her head and stared at her sister. "Um, what the actual fuck, Katrina? How does your mind land on such conclusions with no prompting even?"

Katrina let out a belly laugh. "See, aren't you glad you came out with me?"

"I'm certainly amused now that I came out with you. And I fear my story is going to pale in comparison to your imagination. Maybe you should be writing my book for me."

"Thanks, but I'll take a hard pass on that. I'm much better teaching third graders."

"Are you, though? When you have notions about pornos popping into your head out of nowhere like that? Is that so good for the younger generation?"

"You're just jealous I have a more vivid imagination than you do."

"Yeah, well, it would take a hell of an imagination to get to where you landed with what I was about to tell you."

"Which was?"

"Well, you were two years younger than me, so you probably don't even remember this at all, but there was this really gross kid named Josh Trumbull in my class—"

"Ha ha! The Mad Farter! He also used to eat his boogers in the lunchroom. I totally remember him. He was hysterical."

Alyssa blanched. "He was decidedly not hysterical, Katrina. He was despicable."

Kat pretended she was holding a teacup with her pinky out. "Oh, you prim and proper Miss Priss, get real. It was so damned funny when he did the things he did. He was a doofy little kid trying to get your attention."

"*My* attention?"

"Of course, your attention. Do you remember when you were in middle school, there was a rumor that he was going to ask you to some dance and you freaked out and told Caitlyn Colby to put the word out that he'd better not dare ask you?"

Alyssa furrowed her brow. "I did?"

"You sure did. And when Mom got wind of it, you were in so much trouble?"

"Are you sure you're talking about me?"

"Honey, I was younger than you, but I wasn't stupid. I think you must've been in eighth grade so I was in sixth. It wasn't a big school. Word got out. Everyone was blabbing about it."

Alyssa's eyes grew wide. "Did I black that out of my memory? I was certain I never dealt with him again after Caitlyn's party and the spin the bottle incident."

Kat laughed. "Oh my God, that was such a funny story."

Alyssa glared at her. "It was not even remotely funny. It

was mortifying."

"Okay so maybe when you were whatever, eight or nine—" She shoveled a forkful of fried rice into her mouth. "Mmm... Delicious."

"Try ten—"

"All right. Ten. So you're ten and the dumb boy farts and blames you, but that's what dumb boys did when they were that age. I'd have probably peed my pants laughing at that."

The chef started clanging his spatula and they looked up—he was preparing to fling bits of food at them to catch.

"Focus," Alyssa said. "This is my favorite part."

The chef wound up and banged one spatula against the other to launch a piece of shrimp in the air toward her sister, who dodged and weaved her head and caught it square on her tongue. The table clapped and she stood up and took a bow. Next, the chef flung another piece of shrimp toward Alyssa. The piece tipped her nose, ricocheted off her wrist, bouncing far enough back in her mouth that she had a choking fit, which drew the attention of half the restaurant. Finally she hacked the piece out and everyone clapped for her.

"Well, that was mildly embarrassing," she said.

"Hey, I think everyone was more impressed with how you caught that thing than concerned about the choking episode."

Alyssa rolled her eyes. Choking episode. Marvelous.

"But in the meantime, you still haven't told me whatever it is your deep, dirty secret was that was so embarrassing."

"We're circling the wagon train with this dull story," Alyssa said, popping a piece of her hibachi chicken into her mouth. "Have I said how freaking amazing this stuff is?"

Kat rubbed her belly. "I'd totally put one of these in my

house if I were to build my own place. Imagine having this for dinner every night. With sake." She winked and took a big gulp. "Okay, now back to the story."

"So my doorbell rings a couple of weeks ago and lo and behold, who is it but none other than Josh Trumbull."

"The Mad Farter? What was he doing at your door?"

"He's my new general contractor, you ding-dong!"

Kat started to laugh. "That is so perfect. All these years of unrequited love and voilà, he shows up on your doorstep?"

Alyssa shook her head. "Unrequited love? You are so nuts, sister. I never loved him. I didn't even like him."

"Yeah, but he loooooved you." She wedged her fingertip into her sister's cheek. "Josh and Alyssa, sitting in a tree, K-I-S-S-I-N-G."

Alyssa picked up a piece of her shrimp, prepared to toss it at her sister's face, but then thought better of it because it was far too yummy to waste. Instead she popped it into her mouth.

"So, has he been farting away in your house ever since?"

Alyssa shook her head. "That's the problem. He's been perfectly normal. So normal he almost ignores me. But—not gonna lie—he's freaking gorgeous. And he's in and out of my house with tight Levi's on and a T-shirt that conforms to his strong, muscular chest and arms. He's got a dazzling smile—must've had braces after middle school. And he's an all-around nice guy."

"So? What's the problem?"

"What's the problem? Are you kidding me? He ate flies, Katrina. Flies. He popped them in his mouth."

"I'm gonna go out on a limb and assume they're long since digested. And I'd imagine even if he did have fly breath briefly, that, too, has passed."

"Fly breath? Ugh." Alyssa plugged her nose at the thought. "Honestly, this is one of the weirder conversations we've had over the years."

"But it's cracking me up. I love that this dude showed up at your door. It feels serendipitous."

"Serendipitous that the one male on the planet I vowed never to have contact with again is now traipsing through my life unbidden? Yeah, right."

"All the more delicious. And this is what we were talking about earlier. You. You and your boring, predictable existence. Never going out on a limb. Never doing the very thing you swore you'd never do. And here that thing is right in front of you, challenging you to step out of your little box you drew with black crayon all those years ago and enter into the world filled with all sorts of possibilities!" She leaned over and nudged Alyssa with her elbow. "Or at the very least, maybe some great sex." The older woman sitting next to Katrina stared at her wide-eyed.

"Why on earth would I have sex with the man when I barely speak with him? Besides, I've got a book to write."

"How's that working for you?"

Alyssa thrust out her lower lip. "Not so well. I've been stuck for weeks."

"Honey, you've been stuck for years. Consider Josh Trumbull the antiglue you've needed in your life. The sexy, muscular, blue jeans-clad superhot piece of ass who is going to unstick you." She motioned to the waitress for two more sakes, which the woman promptly delivered.

"We're going to need a team of sled dogs to haul me out of here if I consume that thing."

Kat held up the little carafe of the strong rice wine. "To liquid courage."

"What am I supposed to do with that? Go home and

call him and ask him to come over while I'm stinking drunk so I can have my wicked way with him?"

"Oh gosh, no. I want you to be one hundred percent stone-cold sober when you straddle Josh Trumbull in the hot tub."

Alyssa glanced at the woman on the other side of her sister, who looked at her with her mouth agape. "Straddling him in the hot tub is a euphemism," Alyssa said to her. "It's kind of a joke. I don't even know him. I could never straddle him in the hot tub." The woman shifted her eyes back and forth and pursed her lips until a teenage boy to her left tugged her arm and pulled her away from her eavesdropping venture.

"Now you have total strangers thinking that I'm some kind of porn queen, Katrina! I'm so mortified!"

"Yeah well, you being mortified got you into this spot to begin with. Just think if you'd never been embarrassed by Josh back when you were in elementary school. You two could've hooked up back then—"

"I can assure you ten-year-olds don't hook up—"

Kat waved her hand. "Yeah, yeah, I meant that figuratively. You could've smooched and held hands and gone steady and you'd never have grown up to be so uptight and rigid."

Alyssa's eyes opened wide. "Uptight and rigid? I'm neither of those things!"

Katrina lifted one eyebrow. "So in your last book, you had this love story with these two people and did they even once have sex?"

Alyssa frowned. "It didn't move the story forward."

"You're telling me that sex doesn't move a story forward? How does one have a relationship with someone and not have it result in sex—and pretty early on in the relationship for that matter? And doesn't that advance their relationship a whole lot?"

"Ugh. I have no interest in writing sex scenes in my books. I want people to go along having antiseptic relationships and they can do that stuff behind closed doors, thank you."

"Maybe that's why you're so stuck trying to write this book. 'Cause you know you're skipping over the good bits, the real truth in the story."

"When did you get to be all 'porn stories' and 'sex scenes'?"

"When did you get so uptight about that?"

Alyssa paused. Huh. That was a good question. It wasn't like she hadn't had her share of superficial relationships with guys she'd slept with. Wasn't that what college was all about? But then she kind of turned into a loner. Her friends had all gotten serious boyfriends—even Caitlyn was married now— so she didn't do much except work, and she worked alone. She had zero interest in going on dating apps. That was too awkward. "I'm not uptight. I'm not... anything."

"So then it's time for you to be *something*, Alyssa. You're young and smart and fun and gorgeous. You should be sharing your gifts, not hiding them. I've got an assignment for you: you need to hook up—finally!—with that handsome general contractor of yours."

"Handsome? You don't even know what he looks like. How would you know if he's handsome?"

"Well, I do remember what he looked like when we were kids, and he had all the potential to look pretty awesome as a man. And besides, you told me so, you dingus."

Alyssa pursed her lips. She had, hadn't she? And she also mentioned nothing about his building skills, only about how he fit his clothes. "How do you propose I go about doing this? Walk up to him and say something like 'Is that a hammer in your pocket or are you just happy to see me?'"

Her sister belted out a laugh. "Oh my God, that is so perfect. I would pay good money to watch you say that. Seriously."

Alyssa rolled her eyes. "But seriously, though."

"Use your imagination! I know you have one—I mean, you do write books for a living. Let it happen organically. And then orgasmically." She started laughing again.

Alyssa caught the eye of the eavesdropping gal and rolled her eyes. "She's talking about organic gardening. Really." She lightly punched her sister in the arm.

"So, when he shows up and you don't know what to do and you're feeling kind of stupid, then think about how much more fun it will be when it does happen orgasmically. That should give you some ideas, not to mention some motivation."

Alyssa heaved a sigh. "For sure. I mean, what could go wrong, right?"

She had no choice but to give it a go.

Chapter Six

JOSH knocked on the door and rang the bell, but no one answered. Alyssa had given him a key in case she wouldn't be home, but it was eight in the morning, so he couldn't imagine she'd gone out. Maybe she was on a run. Oh well, he had a lot to do and might as well let himself in. After he stepped inside and removed his boots, he heard a loud noise down the hall and figured he should check that Alyssa was okay.

Her bedroom door was wide open, and holy shit, there she lay, splayed out on her bed in the tiniest T-shirt, sound asleep, snoring away, her hand unmistakably positioned inside her panties, between her legs as if she'd been pleasuring herself. The noise was coming from her laptop which was plugged in next to her on the bed, blasting the telltale sounds of a couple having sex.

"You can use your tool on me any time," a woman said with breathy anticipation. "Go on, drill that cock into me."

The guy, wearing a construction hat, no shirt, and jeans unzipped with his huge cock stroking her slit, said something about nailing studs, and she praised his shaft. He glanced at the browser and saw she'd pulled up a porn site called Hard Hats.

Huh. Had Little Miss Uptight fallen asleep rubbing one out while fantasizing about fucking her contractor? He was so caught up with having stumbled upon her red-handed, he hadn't thought to fully take in the sight before him until now: Alyssa Heyward, a vision of unbelievable beauty—not to mention his ultimate fantasy—as close to naked as he'd probably ever get to see, her blond hair spread out around her head like a halo, her generous breasts soft beneath the thin shirt, her long legs spread wide enough to give him a little view of what he'd been missing out on all these years. He could tell she didn't do the Brazilian thing, which was curious to him—most women he'd been with were waxed bare. Which was fun, but it was intriguing to know that beneath that gruff exterior lay a bush waiting for his hungry cock to explore. God, the idea of sliding his dick inside her, that hairy pussy swallowing it up, made him crazy. He needed to get out of this room. If she woke to find him staring at her box, he was fucked. And not in the way he so needed to be. Shit. How was he ever going to look at her again without getting the hardest of hard-ons?

Josh was relieved he'd taken off his boots—he'd never complain about that again—and was able to slowly back out of the bedroom, leaving Alyssa none the wiser that he'd borne witness to her most private of moments. And now he had hope because maybe Alyssa Heyward was as horny for him as he was for her. There was only question though: how could he unlock this sexy little temptress so they could stop playing silly games with no winners… and finally start playing games that both of them could win?

Alyssa woke to the sound of a sledgehammer. For a minute, she was unsure whether the sledgehammer was perhaps inside her skull because of the powerful throb that reverberated in her head. Shit. What had she done to deserve this?

Her parched tongue felt glued to the roof of her mouth. And one glance down there told her how she'd fallen asleep last night. The other huge clue was a porn video that must've been playing on a replay loop somehow throughout the night. And it all started to come back to her: how Kat persuaded her she needed to come on to her childhood nemesis. How Kat had ordered a second round of those huge carafes of sake, and then for some godforsaken reason had ordered another round. And at that point, Alyssa had decided that made sense.

She had a vague recollection of the Uber driver—a woman named Vixen, if she heard it right—helping her into the house and Alyssa thanking her an embarrassing number of times and promising a rave review on the app. Shit, she probably hadn't even locked the door before she went to bed and got off fantasizing about Josh. Josh. Oh crap. Josh. All that pounding must mean he'd already arrived and gotten to work. Had he seen her? God, no. He wouldn't do that, would he? She needed to shower, revive her miserably hungover head, attempt to work, and figure out how to use her awkwardly unfeminine lack of wiles to make Josh think of her as something other than his cranky customer. Starting now.

She had to forego her run—no way could she even think of doing that with her current alcohol-muddied mental state. But a shower and a couple of ibuprofen would go far toward reviving her. And maybe give her a chance to call upon her inner temptress.

After padding down the hall to the bathroom, she took care of business and brushed her teeth, then opened the curtains and left the door open a bit. To keep the room from steaming up, of course. She turned on the water, pulled off her T-shirt, slipped her panties down, and opened the clear glass shower door, closing it loudly behind her. Maybe Josh's curiosity would get the better of him and he'd come see what the noise was.

She let the hot water stream over her body for a few minutes and finally felt a little more human. Pouring shampoo into her hand, she lifted her arms and scrubbed and rinsed her hair. She applied conditioner through her tangles and lathered up a washcloth and slicked it across her skin, lifting one leg, then the other, washing between her legs as well. She had no idea if Josh was watching, but it kind of turned her on to think he could be. The feeling of the washcloth caressing her labia made her remember last night, as she watched the "construction worker" and his "customer." The whole time, she kept seeing Josh's face instead of the guy on the screen, and she imagined she was the one he was bending over and sliding inside. Hanging up the washcloth, she leaned under the stream of water, lifting her arms again to rinse the conditioner from her hair. Soon she found her hands sliding down her wet body, her fingers toying with her nipples, then sliding farther down between her legs. She swirled her finger around her clit, gathering the building moisture from her opening to slick her fingers more easily. She moaned, thinking about what it would be like if Josh's fingers were sliding along her lips, then up inside her wet pussy. With a moan, she felt the orgasm take hold, the waves of spasms rushing over her.

"Oh, Josh, right there," she cried out as her climax wrung out the last contractions. She stood under the rapidly cooling water, her eyes closed, wondering if she'd had an audience. And kind of freaking out that she took it way too

Hard to Get Lucky

far by invoking his name in the heat of passion.

Chapter Seven

NEVER in his life had Josh thought he'd have the desperate need to jack off not once but twice before lunchtime. On a job site. But when he heard the shower running, followed by the shower door slamming shut, he couldn't help but sneak over there in case Alyssa was putting on a show. My God, what a show it was. Had she left the door open on purpose, hoping he'd watch her? Did she like that, hoping—or better still knowing—he was watching? This little cat-and-mouse thing had him seriously hot and bothered.

Once she'd lifted her arms to shampoo her hair, the sight of her tits, high and perky, enthralled him. God, he wanted so badly to settle his mouth over first one, then the other nipple and suck on them, hard. As she moved her way down her body, soaping and scrubbing, it was all he could do to not strip off his clothes and join her.

When she'd finished rinsing her hair and slid her hands down her body, playing with her nipples, he'd actually moaned. Out loud. It was amazing she didn't hear him. If he wasn't so afraid of getting caught, he'd have unzipped his jeans and pulled out his cock and come in unison with her. Ahhh, and when she came, she moaned so loudly, her body trembling from the aftershocks. And she'd shouted out his name—she'd been fantasizing that he was the one who'd brought her to climax.

Now he knew: Getting her into his bed, and even better,

his life was no longer a matter of if, but when. In the meantime, he deserved an Academy Award nomination for his acting skills. For the rest of the day, he pretended he was unaware of what had gone on, feigning he was busy working, when all he could do was think about how badly he needed to get into her pants, and fast. He'd have one terrible case of blue balls until he could get home and relieve himself of the sexual tension of the past hour or so.

Once she got through the worst of the hangover, Alyssa spent the rest of the morning and well into the afternoon writing. It had been the first time in weeks that she was motivated to get the words down, and she felt good. Shortly after four in the afternoon, her doorbell rang and she found her sister standing at the door.

"Kat? What're you doing here?"

Her sister pushed past her into the foyer. "I'm here to see you-know-who, of course!" She looked to the left, then to the right. "Where is he?"

Alyssa held her finger to her lips. "Shush! He's going to hear you!"

"Oh, I'm sure he's busy using his tool and can't hear me!"

Alyssa smacked her. "Shut up!"

"You just want him to use his tool on you, don't you?"

"Oh my God, I am going to kick you out of this house this instant—"

"Josh! It's me, remember? Katrina?"

Alyssa turned to see Josh in all his sweaty hotness

stretching out his arm to shake hands with her sister. At least he hadn't attempted to hug her. Jesus, what had come over her? She'd morphed from sworn enemy to brooding wannabe love interest in the blink of a damned eye. This was all Kat's fault. She'd planted the seed in her mind. And now her own damned hormones were harvesting the latent desire. Oy, she was so screwed.

"Katrina Heyward, it's been a long time! What have you been up to?"

"Keeping busy, teaching little kids to become good citizens of the globe, being a sister whisperer, that sort of thing."

He arched a brow. "Sister whisperer?"

Alyssa shook her head. "Don't ask." She started trying to corral her sister back out the door she'd come in from.

"Aww, Lyss, I don't want to leave yet. Me and Joshy were getting caught up."

Alyssa shot her sister a hard side-eye that said in no uncertain terms she would sneak into her home when she least expected it and shave her eyebrows off if she didn't stop immediately.

"So, look at the time," Alyssa said, pointing at her watch. "Don't you have a spin class to go to, or yoga, or better yet, a self-introspection course to attend?"

Kat shrugged. "I got nothing. My night is wide open."

Alyssa smiled without revealing any teeth. She was so going to kill Katrina as soon as she had the chance. "Ah. Great."

"In fact, I was going to suggest we all go out and get some beers and nachos and catch up a little bit."

Alyssa turned so her back was facing Josh and mouthed to her sister, "Beer and nachos? What the hell?"

"Josh? You free?"

He nodded. He nodded! "Sure. Sounds like fun. Give me ten minutes to put my tools away and I'll even drive."

Alyssa waited for Josh to go out the back door before freaking out on her sister. "What the hell, Kat?"

"Just giving you a friendly little shove in the right direction. A little sister whispering, if you will."

"Did I look like I needed help?"

Kat shook her head and rolled her eyes. "You've looked like you've needed help with this for a long damned time. Remember? We're getting you out of that black box you drew for yourself."

"You're starting to bug the shit out of me, you know?"

"That's what little sisters are for."

Josh reappeared. "Ready when you are."

Kat reached over and linked her arm through his, pushing Alyssa to do the same on his other side. With her sister acting like some sort of social life conductor, Alyssa felt like a fool.

Out front, Josh opened the passenger side of his truck.

"Oh, I drove here, so I'll drive separately," Katrina said. "Go on, Alyssa. You ride up there with Josh."

Alyssa mouthed the words "I'm going to kill you" for good measure.

"Meet you both at that new brewery over in Springfield, near the Metro stop?"

Kat lived a few minutes away from there, which meant afterward, she'd no doubt shoo Alyssa off with Josh and leave them in that awkward position of wondering *What's next?*

The two of them arrived first and found a table outside, where they ordered drinks and appetizers.

"I haven't been here before," he said, admiring the beer garden. It was hard to feel as if you weren't in generic suburbia in most of Northern Virginia, so to be in a charming, enclosed beer garden complete with hanging baskets overflowing with bright red and pink and purple geraniums almost made you feel as if you were in Germany. Almost.

Luckily Katrina's arrival interrupted any awkwardness of sitting with Josh. He stood when she was about to sit, which was a charming little courtesy that Alyssa enjoyed seeing.

"We took the liberty of ordering for you," he said as the beers arrived along with the first of the appetizers.

"So, Josh, what have you been up to all these years?"

He took a deep breath. "Well, it's an awful lot of years to account for. After high school, I attended Tech for undergraduate and got into woodworking for fun while I was there. By the time I graduated, I was so busy with woodworking jobs, I had to turn down work. I'd studied to be an engineer, so it was a strange path I followed instead. First I was doing woodworking, then cabinetry in custom homes, and after that, people started asking me to take on their construction projects. It all kind of happened organically."

The two women glanced at each other from the side and burst out laughing.

He cocked his head. "Something I missed?"

"Ignore that," Alyssa said. "It's a stupid inside joke from my sister, who loves to make dumb jokes. Nothing to do with you whatsoever."

"It's true. I'm the big prankster and can't help but amuse myself at all the wrong times."

Alyssa kicked her sister's foot under the table and Kat yelled out, "Ouch!"

"Everything okay?" he asked.

Hard to Get Lucky

Alyssa waved her hands. "Sorry I must've stepped on Kat's foot by accident."

"So, Katrina, you're saving the world, one child at a time, I gather," he said with a grin. "And even though I've been working at the house for a few weeks now, I still know nothing about how you became a writer, Alyssa."

"My sister can't help but hide her light under a bushel," Kat said.

Of course, Alyssa knew it was more like she'd been hiding from Josh since the minute he'd shown up at her house. Perhaps she'd done so because deep down she couldn't trust herself around him. Meanwhile she now practically craved him. Curse her darned sister. Had she not shown up, he'd have gone home and Alyssa could have focused on writing her book and going to bed. Instead she was mere feet away from him, feeling a warm rush of embarrassment (or was it yet more horniness?) at his paying attention to her.

"It's nothing all that exciting," she said. "I was working in marketing and communications and didn't love my job. There was no room for advancement—my boss had been there for fifteen years and wasn't going anywhere. So each day after I finished my work but before I could leave for the day, I starting writing my novel, chapter by chapter."

"Cool."

"And all of a sudden, I had an entire book written."

"And she asked me to read it," Kat said. "And I was blown away by it. I reached out to a friend from school who was working in publishing and got her to pass it on to an agent she knew and voilà—"

"We ended up having a couple of publishing houses fighting over the rights to the book, which was pretty cool."

"Which meant good money for Lyss, luckily."

"And then the book came out to great reviews and sold lots of copies and then another that sold well, and now I am. Stuck."

He frowned. "Stuck?"

She nodded. "Yup. I haven't been able to figure out this story like I did with the last two books. It's not coming to me. I can't get into writing it, so I spend hours staring at my computer screen."

"I told her she needs to have her characters have sex."

"Is this a normal discussion, suggesting imaginary people have imaginary sex so that, what?" Josh lifted his eyebrow as he spoke.

"So that it's more interesting, of course." Kat took a swig of her beer. "I mean, isn't everything in life more interesting with sex in it?"

A rush of heat traveled up Alyssa's chest, neck, and face. Sometimes she wondered if Katrina was even related to her—they were so different. Often, Kat seemed casual about discussing things Alyssa considered private.

"I'm not going to raise any objections to more sex," he said, grabbing a chip and biting into it. "I wouldn't be a guy if I wasn't in favor of more sex, whichever way it happened."

Kat turned to her. "See? We both agree you need to make your characters get it on. Then you'll get your groove back with your book and finish it in no time."

"Kat, weren't you supposed to stop and pick up some groceries to take to Mom's tonight?"

Katrina squinted at her. "Ahhh, yes. I almost forgot about that. I best be hitting the road or she won't have ingredients to make dinner."

Alyssa made a move to stand, but her sister pushed her back down. "Don't leave on my account."

"You know I need to go home and put in a few hours

of work."

Kat turned to Josh. "I tell her all work and no play makes Alyssa a horny girl, but she won't listen."

Alyssa did a spit take with her beer on that remark. "Forgive my sister for her one-track mind. I think we need to find her some companionship. Either that or some upscale reading material."

"The kind where the characters don't have sex? No thanks. Bo-ring." She pretended to yawn. "Josh, you mind bringing Alyssa back home?"

"Happy to," he said. "It's right on my way."

He asked the waitress for the check and settled up, and Alyssa climbed back into the car for what she knew would be an awkward drive home. No thanks to nosy Katrina.

Chapter Eight

"WELL, your sister sure is a spitfire." He was tempted to say horndog with sex-on-the-brain, but didn't want to be too judgy.

"Let's just say she means well but sometimes loves to stick her nose where it doesn't belong."

"I get that. But I'm jealous you have a sister to be nosy with."

"You're an only child?"

He nodded. "My folks didn't stick around long enough to create any other kids. One and done, and then my dad was outta there."

She reached over and put her hand on top of his, which had been resting on his thigh. The feeling of her warm hand on his stirred his blood. And he hoped it wasn't stirring the sleeping giant awake again. He still hadn't taken care of that problem from earlier in the day. If he wasn't careful, he'd embarrass himself right here and now.

"Thanks. Not gonna lie—it was pretty awful when I was a kid. But I guess I eventually got used to it."

"Intellectually, maybe, but I don't think you can ever get over the loss of a parent—either from abandonment or losing them unexpectedly."

He thought about that for a second. "I suppose you're right. There's always a black hole there that doesn't seem to get filled up. What about you? You mentioned your mother.

What about your dad?"

"He died when I was in college—heart attack. Very sudden. He was here, then he was gone. I think the hardest thing was never being able to say goodbye, or not remembering when it was I last said 'I love you.' It's all so, well, permanent."

Taking a chance, he turned his hand so that he could link fingers with her. Such a tiny thing but it felt like a bold move, one he wouldn't have taken a day ago. Yet now that he suspected she might welcome the gesture, he figured, *Why not?*

"I'm so sorry that happened, Alyssa. You didn't deserve that."

"I'm sorry I never knew about your parents. That must've been tough, you being an only child."

He nodded. "I guess I compensated. Acted like a jackass in school. I wanted attention so much I'd do anything—even super stupid things—to get it."

She grinned. "You? Do stupid things? I can't recall."

He gave her a joking punch in the arm. "Nice try."

"Well, I wasn't quite sure how to broach that subject."

"You mean of me being a total fool?" They pulled up in front of her house. "Looks like this is your stop."

"You want to come in? I'm not sure what I've got in the kitchen, but I'm sure I can throw on a pot of spaghetti or something pretty easily."

"Considering all I have in my fridge is a carton of old milk, one egg, and a container of guacamole, I'd love an actual home-cooked meal."

"Home-cooked might be a stretch, but let's see what we can rustle up."

He hopped out of the truck and came around to open her door. "Let me know what I can do to help out."

Once inside, she scavenged about her food pantry, pulling out some shallots and lemons and butter, chicken stock, and arborio rice. "How does risotto sound? I've got some shrimp in the freezer I can defrost quickly and sauté. Maybe serve it up with a little salad?"

"That sounds like the best meal I've had in months. Now put me to work."

She pulled out lettuce, a cucumber, carrots, celery, and cherry tomatoes and handed them to him to fix the salad.

"Here's a knife and a cutting board. Good luck."

They set about their duties, with Mo coming in to do figure eights around their ankles while they cooked and prepped.

"If you could grab a can of cat food—and there's where the spoons are—and scoop it into Mo's bowl, she will be forever indebted to you."

"No problem." He took care of the cat's dinner, finished up the salad, and came up behind Alyssa, who'd been at the stove stirring things for the past twenty minutes.

He leaned over, his face near hers, his nose by her neck. "Smells amazing," he said, inhaling deeply. He wasn't sure if he was referring to her or the food she was cooking. Then he reached around and covered her stirring hand with his, the two of them sharing a spoon and stirring the rice as each scoop of hot broth cooked into it.

"You have a magic touch with this," he said.

"I think it's you who's cast a spell in here."

"To the contrary, Alyssa. You cast a spell on this boy long, long ago." He leaned down and pressed his nose to the back of her head, breathing in the scent of the shampoo he'd watched her work into her hair that morning. It made him lightheaded to think back to that magical moment when he saw her there, beams of morning light shining through the window, highlighting the erotic scene unfolding before him.

Pushing things made him nervous, but how could he not? He was here now, with her, his body pressed up to hers, and he knew she could feel his hard cock growing each minute they stood so closely. Taking the risk, he reached over and turned off the stove then burrowed his nose in her hair and moved down toward her neck. As he reached around and found her breasts, he groaned as his lips trailed along her neck, along her jawbone, at last finding her lips as she turned her head to receive him.

The room was silent but for their breathing and the sound of their lips and mouths tangling for the first time as they tried to find their rhythm. Their tongues mated and twined. Alyssa moaned, which he took as a sign of encouragement, so he turned to face her and grabbed her by the waist, lifting her up so she could wrap her legs around him, their lips not separating. He shifted away from the stove and carried her to the bar counter and settled her on it as he reached for her top and pulled it off quickly.

Stopping for a moment, he took in the view: this woman he'd craved for so long, here before him, her breasts confined by nothing more than a tiny black bra. He reached behind her and slipped loose the hooks of her bra, then tugged the straps down as she shook her arms loose of the thing. His mouth dropped open as he stared at her luscious breasts, her high, pink nipples already hard with excitement. When he settled his mouth over one, she groaned in pleasure, causing his cock to strain almost painfully in his jeans. He reached down and unbuttoned and lowered the fly, providing temporary relief, giving him a chance to focus on her as he nipped and licked and sucked on first one nipple, then the other. Alyssa threw her head back as he played with them, encouraging him with the sounds of her pleasure.

"Oh God, Josh, right there. More, harder."

He needed to have her against him, flesh on flesh. Tugging at his T-shirt, he pulled it over his head, then pulled her off the counter to work the buttons of her jeans. He couldn't think straight and wanted to be inside her so badly. After he shimmied her jeans down along her thighs, he left her standing before him in sheer black panties and nothing else. He thought he'd died and gone to heaven.

"Well, don't make me be the only one standing here in just this," she said and pushed his jeans down. He bent over to unlace his boots and kicked them off, then shrugged off the jeans at his ankles and found himself face-to-face with those sheer black panties. He skimmed them off and lifted her up again onto the counter, then spread her open wide so he could explore her with his lips and tongue.

"Ooohhh God. Josh. That is amazing."

Circling his tongue along her clit, he dragged long, lazy strokes along her pussy lips and back again. He couldn't get over the smell of her, the taste of her, that here he was, licking the very pussy he was eyeing this morning with unrequited lust.

It wasn't long till he knew Alyssa was on the edge, her body trembling, her moans coming faster. He inserted first one, then two fingers inside her as he licked along her lips and circled her clit again. She broke, long and loud, the muscles inside her pussy contracting over his fingers as she convulsed in pleasure.

As soon as she came down from her climax, he pulled her back against his waist, his swollen cock nudging against her. He pressed her back into the kitchen wall and slid her down on top of his hard dick, gasping at the feel of her warm, wet pussy swallowing him up. Once seated deep inside her, he waited for a minute, relishing the feel of finally being home. But he couldn't wait long; he needed to come, and bad. Soon he lifted her off his cock and began pumping in and out of her, leaning his mouth down to suck on a nipple, then returning to her mouth, then back again. He was crazed with lust, with the heat and the slick glide of her body fluids easing his cock in and out of her.

"Oh my God, I'm gonna come again," she said, gasping for air.

"Come with me, Lyss." He thrust his cock deep inside of her once, twice, and a third time before his seed came pouring out of him deep inside her warm body. He could feel her body jerking as his did, and she called out his name, sated.

It seemed forever till Josh had his wits about him; he had no clue how he'd remained standing with their bodies still connected.

He pressed his forehead to hers. "Holy shit, Alyssa Heyward," he said, gasping for air. "That was worth the wait."

Chapter Nine

ALYSSA remained seated on Josh's cock, their fluids merging as he slipped from her pussy. That's when it hit her—she'd had unprotected sex with this man she both knew but didn't know. Didn't know in that she had no idea if he practiced safe sex. She practiced the safest of sex, since she never had any with anyone anyhow. She wasn't worried about getting pregnant, since she'd remained on the pill once she'd gotten on it—she'd always thought it was too much of a pain to stop, only to find you needed it again.

Josh had started to kiss her again, planting soft, tender kisses all over her face. He walked them both down the hall, into her bedroom, and onto her bed, where only this morning she'd awoken with a raging hangover and sticky fingers, having passed out the night before with her hand between her legs, watching fantasy porn about having sex with your builder. How very meta of her. Life imitating art imitating life. Or something like that. Although not like she'd ever consider porn art. But that was a debate for another day.

She was torn between wanting to go for round two and being slightly appalled that she'd caved so readily even before they'd had a proper meal.

Josh, however, had drifted off to sleep, it seemed. His eyes were closed and his breathing was soft and gentle. He'd pulled Alyssa up against his chest minutes before, so she wasn't going anywhere. Nor did she want to. She was surprisingly happy right where she was.

Turns out he was only taking a refresher nap, and ten minutes later, he was kissing her again.

He rolled her over so that he was on top of her, but she soon rolled them both over and straddled him.

"According to my sister, the goal was for me to straddle you, albeit in the hot tub," she said with a grin.

"I didn't know your sister had a say in this."

"I may have mentioned she's a bit meddlesome." She grinned. "And she somehow decided that I needed to step out of my comfort zone and have sex with you."

He arched an eyebrow. "She did, did she?" He reached up and plucked at her nipples. "And how did she even know of my existence?"

"I told her you were working on the renovation project."

"Does that mean she encourages you to have sex with any workers who come to your home?"

Alyssa swatted at him. "Only the ones I shunned in childhood, apparently."

"About that—"

"I need to apologize to you about that, Josh," she said. "It was all very weird, you know? I was young and naïve and I'd never had an experience like that. And then, I mean, you did do some things that I couldn't comprehend."

"The fly."

She nodded.

"The flatulence."

"That was practically a #MeToo moment in that storage room, you know." She pressed her lips into a frown. "If that had happened now, I'd have reported you to the authorities."

He laughed, that grin of his cocked a little sideways as

he glanced at her from the corner of his eye, a look that slayed her. "It's funny to picture stupid me as a dumb ten-year-old being hauled off in cuffs for trying so hard to get you to kiss me."

"Kiss that fly breath of yours?" She smiled. "I'd rather challenge someone to an anchovy-eating contest, thanks."

They kissed some more and Alyssa took advantage of her position by stroking herself along Josh's hardening cock. Her breathing became labored, as did his, and she shifted so that his cock could slide inside her. It was her turn to settle on top of him with his cock as deep as it could be.

"I wish I'd have known then how amazing this would feel," she said. "I wouldn't have wasted all that time."

He laughed. "Hate to tell you but that would have been far more than a #MeToo moment. I'd have been hauled off to prison for sure."

She reached out and clasped hands with his as she lifted herself off him and slid back down again, riding him like a horse.

"The good news is now there are no rules or restrictions, and we can play to our heart's content."

Taking him in at this angle felt especially good, like it was hitting her G-spot or something, plus she could stroke her clit with every glide and press of her body. Soon she felt the familiar stirring in her pelvis, the sensation of his swollen head reaching deep enough to press her cervix, her clit sliding along his cock. It was all too much. Stars burst behind her eyelids and she thrashed her hips against his, trying to have him as deep as she could. In seconds, he flipped her, reaching for her legs to spread her wide, hooking them through his arms as he pressed hard and deep into her, his orgasm looming, his body tightening, and the rush of come shooting in spurts deep within her.

Hard to Get Lucky

God, Josh never knew how amazing sex could be with the right person. But how would he know she was the right person, having been with her for a mere few hours?

They slept on and off for the rest of the night, barely able to keep their hands off each other for more than an hour or so.

At seven, his phone alarm went off in the kitchen; he could hear it buzzing against the floor from the pocket of his pants. He got up to shut it off and visit the bathroom, then came back to bed.

"You have to wake up for something?" she said, bleary-eyed.

"Gotta get up for work. Though not too far a commute today."

"Come back to bed. We have many more positions to try out."

"Ahh, but my boss is a taskmaster and if I'm late, she'll have my head."

She leaned over and reached for his cock, sticking her tongue out to swipe along the length of it. "Well, I do kinda like this head."

"Hard to believe that only twenty-four hours ago I found you sleeping in this very bed—"

She sat up. "You what?"

Well, shit. That was an unnecessary admission. "Yeah, when I tried to get in, the front door was locked and you didn't answer, so I came in through the back and heard noises down here. I popped my head in to be sure you were okay. Your laptop was on or something and you were sound asleep."

She stared at him. "You saw me like that? You mean that all along, all day long yesterday, you knew how I'd slept the night before? And the porn ''

He winced. "If it helps at all, I found it flattering."

"So like this is some sort of setup, and after that, you schemed to get into my bed? Like I was an easy target or something?" She stood up, hands on her hips—naked, which was making him crazy—and pointed to the door. "Leave, Josh. Now."

He took one look at her face and knew there was no changing her mind. She seemed pissed and embarrassed, and he'd learned long ago how poorly she handled humiliation. Only now that he'd had a taste of Alyssa Heyward, he wasn't giving up that easily.

Chapter Ten

ALYSSA wasn't sure if she was more pissed that Josh didn't come back to work on her house today, or that he'd witnessed what he'd witnessed yesterday and never said a damned thing to her. What was with that guy and humiliating her one way or another? Here he thought she was some Easy Ellen or something—note to self, figure out a better phrase than Easy Ellen—and he figured it was a quick way to get laid? Well, fuck him for that! And she didn't even use a condom. But damn, it felt so much better that way, even for her.

Ugh, what had she gotten herself into? She was smart to have steered clear of Josh Trumbull in the first place—he was nothing but trouble for her.

She'd sat down at her laptop about ten different times during the day, all ready to crank out a couple thousand words, only to find that once again, the words were no longer coming to her. As a thought experiment, she stepped up the sexual tension between her two main characters. In her mind, it was irrelevant to the storyline. Yet no sooner did she ratchet up the sexual tension than the story grew more interesting. Darn that Katrina for being right again.

Not in the mood to learn lessons from her sister, she hit delete on everything she'd changed and called it a day.

The next day, Josh was a no-show again, which was probably for the better. She'd find a new contractor at some point. Yeah, a sledgehammer had already broken through some of her walls, so it wasn't quite as livable, but it was more livable than the alternative: having him there lying through omission about the way he'd found her passed out cold after she masturbated herself to sleep to visions of a professional doppelganger. She felt like such an idiot.

She spent the day writing and deleting and writing and deleting and by the end of the day had deleted more than she'd written, which was a bad sign. She was now officially writing in reverse—in other words, unwriting. Pretty soon she'd have to set up on a street corner with a tin cup to earn her keep if this kept up. Except there weren't any available street corners left. Others had beaten her to them and they weren't gonna give up prime real estate like that to just anyone.

By dinnertime she scoured her cupboard for some semblance of meal-making but found none. The partially cooked risotto mocked her from the container she'd dumped it into in the fridge in between making love with Josh all night long. She shuddered. Making love? Where did she come up with such a term? It was sex, pure and simple. He was scratching her itch and was particularly talented at it.

Crap. She pulled out two pieces of super stale bread, slapped some peanut butter on them, and called it a day. As she crawled into bed, her sister called.

"I'm not interrupting anything, am I?" she said.

"Uh, I was about to file my nails, if that counts. And maybe if I get really wild, I'll brush Mo's coat."

"Wait a minute. Where's Josh? I thought by now you two lovebirds would have set up house—you know, living in a haze of sex, sex, and more sex."

"Uh, no. A hundred percent wrong on that."

"But I'm so good at reading a room and I had the vibes

that you two were hitting it off. I figured you'd go back to your place, maybe grab a bite to eat, and before you knew it he'd be taking you up against the wall."

Huh? This was like one of those things where you mention to someone about one time you saw bourbon glasses etched in octopuses and the next thing you know everything you open on your computer has a damned octopus bourbon glass they're trying to sell you. Even though you never once sought that out—the internet was always watching and listening. And apparently so was Katrina.

"Wait a minute. Did you talk to him? Did Josh call you to complain about me?

"What on earth are you talking about?"

"I mean, you said he was taking me up against the wall. So you must have insider information."

"So he *did* take you up against the wall. See? I knew it! That makes me feel better. I haven't lost my touch."

"For Christ's sake Kat, just because there is a slight chance we possibly had sex up against a wall doesn't mean there was anything more to it."

"So that was it? You fucked, he left, wham, bam, thank you ma'am? Which is okay, 'cause that was our agreement— you could simply do it to do it, nothing more, nothing less. I got the sense that you two liked each other though. Like if we were still in elementary school, you would have sent me a note to send to Josh with something like "Do you like Lyssa? If yes, check here, if no, check here."

"Do you reside in a state of delusion most of the time? Or is this a one-off?"

"I'm going to let that drip off me like water off a duck's back. I know you're lashing out at me because you're probably mad at yourself for something. And my guess is that something has to do with you rejecting Josh. And to be truthful, I'd be mad at you, too, if I knew you'd ditched Josh, 'cause, well, he seems like a sweet guy. And the way he looked at you when you weren't looking."

"He looked at me a certain way?"

"Of course he did."

"Well why didn't you say something?"

"'Cause you kept trying to shut me up, remember?"

"Well, I can't help it. I was under the influence of, of, of something!"

"Love? Lust? Boy crush?"

Boy crush, no doubt. Lust—impossible not to. Love? Was it possible to love someone you knew but then didn't know but then suddenly knew, like in the biblical sense?

"It's complicated, Katrina."

"It's only complicated if you make it so."

"Oh, but I beg to differ with you. You talked me into this crazy plan and I went home drunk and stupid and horny and passed out cold while trying to rub one out to the tune of some porn site for women who get turned on by construction workers."

"About damned time. I think if you did that more often you'd be far, far less uptight."

"Uptight? I am *not* uptight!"

"We're not going to go there right now. But I do need to know: how does what you've told me have any bearing on you and Josh?"

"Because he came in the next morning and heard loud noises in my room and came to check on me and I was still passed out, evidently midwank—does wank count for women, or is that only for men?—with the stupid porn still playing on a repeat loop on my laptop."

Katrina cackled and clapped her hands so loudly Alyssa

could hear it over the phone. "That is super perfect. I must track Josh down and give him props."

"Props? He violated my privacy. He embarrassed me—once again, I might add. He is out of my life, *phhhhhht*! For good!"

"I gotta go, darling. I've got a man to track down. Love ya, bye!"

One of these days, Alyssa was going to throttle that sister of hers.

Chapter Eleven

JOSH took some time off to go fishing, do a little kayaking, and clear his mind. He was suffering from some serious emotional whiplash after the past couple of days. Considering his current work project was at Alyssa's house, he didn't have any other work to do. Might as well chill out and collect his thoughts.

He'd just returned from a quick run to pick up a pizza and some beer when his phone rang. One look at the ID told him it was a blocked number. Weird.

"This is Josh," he said.

"Josh, dude, it's Katrina. We need to talk."

He shook his head. "Nope. We don't."

"Yep, we do. It's about my stupid sister. Well, she's not stupid, but she's acting stupid, which is making me stupid mad at her."

"It's fine, Kat. Really it is. How did you get my phone number?"

"Caitlyn gave it to me, duh."

He rolled his eyes. Caitlyn was always causing him trouble it seemed, even all these years later.

"Look, can we let this go? It didn't work out with me and your sister. That's it."

"Did you or did you not take Alyssa up against her wall?"

Huh? How on earth would she know that? Surely her

sister didn't report back to her about what they did. "I think I'll defer to your sister on that one."

"In which case you did. Okay, good. I knew it. Then I'll extrapolate to presume you then did it ten ways to Sunday over the course of the night, amiright? And in the morning people say stupid things or get crabby or cold feet and it all blows up. My sister is a classic one for cold feet."

"Kat, I need to respect your sister's privacy so I can't explain to you why things fell apart. All you need to know is that they did, and while I would have loved to explore a relationship with Alyssa, it wasn't meant to be. Now, if I can go enjoy my pizza and beer in peace, please?"

"Not quite yet. So I'm going to betray my sister's confidence because sometimes you've gotta do things like that for the betterment of society. 'Cause I'm the one who talked her into living a bit on the edge. I sent her home with stars in her eyes and a plan for seduction—which is *so* not my sister's thing—and the thing is she was super drunk when she decided to, well, warm up to the idea before you were even there."

"Aha… so the shower was your idea?"

"What shower?"

He shook his head. He sure as hell didn't want that one to fall on his head too. "Never mind."

"I'm telling you, Josh, my sister's got it bad for you. And sure, maybe she was a bit embarrassed by the whole construction guy porn thing, but who cares? What you need to do is help her understand that wasn't a bad thing, but a *good* thing."

"Well, of course it was a good thing. You know what a turn-on that was?"

"I'm gonna plug my ears now because this is information that is on a need-to-know basis, 'kay? But I want you to track my sister down and straighten her up. Life's too short for stupid fights about things that don't matter. Plus, I can tell you two are falling in love. Amiright?"

Josh took a look at his pizza and six-pack of beer and sighed. Worst case, she'd throw him out, with the pizza right after him, and it would end up covered in dirt and inedible. As long as she didn't lob beer cans at him, it would be worth the attempt.

The sky was darkening when Josh pulled his truck up in front of Alyssa's house. He grabbed the pizza and beer and walked the gangplank to her doorway and rang the bell. Most likely, she wouldn't even open the door, or better yet, she'd open it for the express purpose of slamming it in his face ten seconds later. He'd never understand women.

It took a few more presses of the doorbell for her to open it the slightest crack, her face wedged between the door and the frame.

Her eyes looked puffy and red. It broke his heart to see she'd been crying, even if it had been self-inflicted. She stood there, not saying a word. Well, this was awkward.

At last, Josh cleared his throat to speak as Mo darted past Alyssa's ankles and out to freedom.

He pointed his thumb over his shoulder. "Uh, you know the cat snuck out?"

Her eyes grew wide. "Mo! She's an indoor kitty and she cost a fortune too. She can't be out there in the dangerous world! Help me get her!"

Without thinking twice, Josh tossed the pizza and beer and took off after the cat, a barefoot Alyssa in hot pursuit.

"Get her, Josh, before she gets hurt!"

"I'm trying. But cats are fast. And I don't want her to think I'm chasing her, either."

They were at a distinct disadvantage as darkness was

settling in fast, and only one of them in the chase had good night vision. The kitty looped and turned. Soon they were heading back in the direction of Alyssa's backyard, where they found a gap in the decorative lattice surrounding the underside of her back deck.

The good news was that unless there were other little gaps on the other side she could sneak out of, she was at least trapped. The bad news? It had rained earlier in the day, and Alyssa had drainage problems in her backyard. Josh would have no choice but to get down and dirty for the cause.

"Okay, before I go under there for her, you need to scout the perimeter of this lattice to be sure she can't get out any other way. I'll stand guard here to be sure the cat doesn't slip back out where she entered."

Alyssa did as she was told and inspected every square inch of the space. "Looks good."

"Okay, then come back here. You're going to have to be the sentry to make sure she doesn't bolt out while I go under to look for her."

They both looked down at the mud puddle exactly where he was going to have to crawl in. He bent down and grabbed a section of the rotting lattice and pulled it away quite readily. Then he pulled his phone out of his pocket and turned the flashlight on, dropped down on his belly, and commando-crawled in the tight space between the deck and the earth toward the kitty who was cowering in the far corner.

"It's okay, kitty. I'm not gonna hurt you," he said in a soothing voice, hoping he'd coax her toward him rather than having to crawl the whole way in the muck and goo to get her. The cat let out a frightened squeak but didn't budge. When he came close to her, she bolted. "Lyssa, grab her quick!" There was no way he could pursue her that fast with only about a foot between him and the deck boards. He had no choice but to reverse crawl back out and hope she'd caught her. Josh heard a squeal, then a woot of joy.

"Got her!" Alyssa said.

"Great! Go get her back inside before she takes off again. I'm too old for this kind of chase."

He slowly extricated himself from the dingy muck, and once cleared of the deck pulled himself up to see he was coated in mud. Could this day get much worse?

He walked around the house to the door and rang the bell again.

Alyssa opened it with Mo wrapped in a towel.

"At least that thing didn't dash out this time."

Alyssa took a look at him and her eyes grew wide. "Oh my. Josh. You're a mess."

"Stating the obvious." He grinned at her.

"Come inside so we can get you cleaned up."

"Can we talk first?"

"Here? Like this?" She pointed at him.

"I need to get some things straightened out, even if I have to do it filthy dirty on your porch stoop."

She shrugged. "I'll defer to you, considering you're the one who looks like the swamp monster." She giggled.

His stomach growled. He glanced over at the box of cold pizza on the lawn. No doubt the ants were having quite a picnic. At least the beers would be intact. After the past few days, he could use a cold beer or two.

"So, look. I know you were really embarrassed when I admitted I'd seen you yesterday morning in the, well, state you were in."

She blushed when he brought it up. "Must we discuss that?"

He nodded. "We absolutely must talk about this. See, you think it's so embarrassing, but baby"—he reached for her hand—"for me it was nothing but a huge turn-on. For my whole life, I thought you hated me. And to realize that you did that because of me?" He grinned. "Hell, I spent the whole morning with a hard-on every time I thought about it—which was pretty much nonstop. It's never a good idea to operate power tools when you're distracted by such things."

"You were turned on? By me?" She looked up at him with wide eyes. "You didn't think that was ridiculous?"

"Ridiculously erotic, maybe." He winked at her. "Speaking of erotic—that shower."

A flush of red washed across her face. "Um…" She bit her lip and it made him want to bite it too.

"You did that on purpose, didn't you?"

"Shower?" She raised her brows.

He reached out and scratched the cat's head while Alyssa hemmed and hawed.

"The one where you opened the curtains and the door and made that loud noise slamming the shower door? So that was a whole setup?"

"Huh, I'm not sure what you're talking about."

"You know, the sensual washing of the hair, your breasts on display to taunt my already hard cock." He took a deep breath. Thinking about it made him hot all over again. "And when you started playing with your tits, pinching your nipples, I thought I was going to go off then. But then you moved your hands down and started stroking yourself and the next thing I knew, you were coming with my name on your lips. Fuck, Alyssa. That killed me. You little tease—I damn near stripped my clothes off and joined you then and there."

"Okay, so maybe it was a little intentional," she said. "I mean, based on past history, I wasn't sure how to go about changing the nature of our relationship. I only knew how to be combative toward you, so I had to try something different. I thought maybe I could use my body to my advantage."

"Jesus, that was the best use of your body I could have ever imagined. Well, until last night."

"About last night—"

"You mean, quite literally, the best night of my life?"

"Are you kidding me?"

He furrowed his brow. "Why would you think that? I would never joke about something as precious as what we had last night. It was, beyond a shadow of a doubt, the most incredible, extraordinary night I've ever had. And the best sex of my life." He continued to pet the cat, all while keeping his muddy distance from Alyssa. "Was it not good for you?"

"It was amazing, Josh. I can't believe I put so much effort into hating you needlessly for so long, when instead I could have had *that*. Which was perfect, by the way."

"Finally, we can agree on something." He took a deep breath.

"Also, I do owe you an apology. I was such a bitch to you. I had no idea what you were going through as a child. I was so caught up in my own drama, I couldn't even bother to consider yours. I was an insensitive kid. Well, a sensitive insensitive kid is more like it. I'm truly sorry."

"Don't worry your pretty head about it for one moment longer," he said, staring into her eyes. He looked down at the cat. "In case you were wondering, this isn't quite the pussy I'd like to be stroking right now, you know." His grin curved up on one side. "My head tells me to pick you up and carry you to your bed so I can have my wicked way with you." He looked down at his clothes. "But my wardrobe is sending off a different vibe."

She pulled him inside and closed the door, dropping the cat on the floor, then lifted his muddy shirt over his head while he made quick work of his pants. Grabbing his hand, she led him down the hall to the bathroom.

"I was thinking perhaps we could kill two birds with one stone—get all that nasty mud off you and maybe enjoy a little command performance from yesterday?"

Josh reached in and turned on the shower. "You don't have to ask twice."

Chapter Twelve

ALYSSA soaped up her hands and worked her magic across Josh's chest, enjoying the feel of her fingers working their way through his chest hair. Soon she slid them lower, across his six-pack abs, reaching around to feel his firm butt, then sliding along his lean hips, following the cut trail that led right where she wanted to be. His cock was already hard as she began to stroke it slowly.

Josh moaned. "Awww, fuck, Alyssa, that's so perfect right there."

He had soaped up his hands as well and used them to circle her nipples before pinching them to make them hard and responsive.

They stood beneath the water playing with each other's bodies, taking their time, exploring, and only when the hot water started to run out did they rinse off.

"As much as I want to take you right here, I think cold water might put a damper on things."

He stepped out of the shower and reached for her hand to help her out, grabbing her towel and tenderly drying her off.

"What kind of hostess am I, not even getting you a towel?"

She reached into the closet, pulled out a towel, and reciprocated, drying him off.

"Could you do me a little favor though?"

He lifted an eyebrow. "You name it."

"Would you mind wrapping that around you, so it hangs low? It's one of those things a girl can never get enough of, seeing her man with a towel simply begging to be ripped off."

He laughed and obliged her, then held his hands up as if modeling himself. "Good enough?"

"Good enough to eat," she said with a wicked grin. "Now, follow me."

She grabbed his hand and led him down the hall to her bedroom. Pulling off the towel, she dropped to her knees, only to see his hard cock spring up in response. Gently, she took him in her hands and proceeded to lick in long, slow strokes up the length of his cock, stopping each time she got to his swollen head and taking it into her mouth to tease him before returning her tongue to the base of his cock. He groaned when she took the length of him into her mouth. She loved the feeling of control she had over his pleasure, the sounds of him moaning as she brought him closer to climax.

Eventually Josh pulled away. "I want to come inside you, baby. Get up there and get on your hands and knees."

Alyssa did as she was told, looking over her shoulder while Josh leaned forward, spreading her open and dragging his tongue along her slit. She couldn't believe the erotic sensations of him licking her from that angle, and she ground herself against his tongue, telling him she wanted more.

At long last, Josh lifted up and moved behind her, sliding his hard cock along her wetness before slipping inside her wet pussy. They both gasped. He leaned forward and wrapped one arm around her waist so his hand could stroke her clit, while the other hand played with her nipple. He started out slowly sliding in, then out, as she savored the sensation of his huge cock spreading her wide. Soon he picked up the pace, and she answered his thrusts with her own, pressing against him, urging him as deep as he could go. Her climax started to work its magic as she lost herself in the sensation of being filled by this incredible man… a man she'd rediscovered and realized she had real feelings for. Plunging his cock in and out, in and out, he pleasured them both. Soon, she yelled out his name. "Josh, come with me, now!" she cried as her pussy spasmed around his cock, and he thrust one last time, his own cock spasming, pumping his come deep inside her. He clutched her around the waist as they both climaxed hard, their sweaty bodies merged together.

Collapsing, they spooned together, sated, and fell into a deep sleep.

A while later, Alyssa's phone rang. She reached for it on the nightstand and saw that it was Katrina calling.

"Should I answer it?" she said sleepily to Josh. "It's my sister."

"Sure. But don't let her know what we've been up to, unless you want it blabbed to the world."

She squeezed his hand. "Yeah?" she said into the phone, which she had pushed to speaker.

"Jesus, Lyss. I've been texting you for hours. I was worried about you. Is everything okay?"

Alyssa looked at Josh lying next to her, tracing lazy circles with his fingers along her belly.

"Everything is just about perfect, Kat. Can't think of a thing I'd change."

With that, she ended the call, set the phone to silent, and returned to the beginning of her new life.

Thank you!

Thank you so much for reading *Hard to Get Lucky!* I hope you enjoyed it! If so, please help others find this book:

1. Help other people find this book by writing a review.

2. Sign up for my new releases email so you can find out about the next book as soon as it's available and get fun giveaways.
    http://eepurl.com/baaewn

3. Like my Facebook page.
    www.facebook.com/jennygardinerbooks

And I love to hear from readers! Let me know what you think about my books! You can write to me at jenny@jennygardiner.net, and visit me on the web at www.jennygardiner.net.

Read on for a teaser of the next book in the Hard to Get series – *Hard to Get Over.*

About *Hard to Get Over*.

Go hard or go home…

After losing her beloved neighbor Violet, Daphne Sweeney realizes her dream when Violet leaves her part ownership of the duplex she shared with her aged friend. Finally, after years of trying to scrape together the money for her own place, Daphne can stay put, establish some real roots, in her humble little home from Violet.

Until she realizes Violet left the remaining ownership of the house to a very distant relative, Brady McGovern, who just so happens to be Daphne's college boyfriend who fled town the day after graduation, never to be heard from again.

And Brady has touched down in town just long enough to unload the property and get back on the road again, just like the good old days.

Read on for a sneak peek.

Chapter One

THERE'S no such thing as a good funeral but if there were, Daphne Sweeney would have had to give herself at least a tiny pat on the back for having executed it. After spending years as a daily lifeline to her elderly neighbor Violet Nicholson, it fell to Daphne to organize the final memorial for Violet, who left behind no living relatives and just a smattering of friends by the time she'd passed in her sleep at the age of ninety-two. Daphne took no pleasure in being the one who'd found her that morning, but felt relief that Violet likely hadn't suffered. It was her first encounter with a dead person and it was a little unsettling for sure. But she immediately took control of the situation, had the appropriate authorities declare Violet officially expired, and then planned the service, which was only attended by a few neighbors who knew her from when she'd sit on the porch stoop and wave to passersby, before she got too old and that task became too onerous.

It was a sobering lesson for Daphne, who'd probably become a bit too much of a homebody over the past couple of years, working at home as a graphic designer since all of her customers were online. It sounded perfect, not having to go to an office, but in reality, she'd kind of lost touch with too many people and instead of taking time off at the end of the workday, discovered herself working too many waking hours. Her work life and personal life (which, let's be honest, was non-existent anyhow) had blurred into one. Seeing how Violet died basically alone was eye-opening to Daphne: did she want to just stumble along into old age, becoming a shut-in, friendless and loveless, void of any romantic relationship, married to her job and not a man who cared about her? She knew that Violet had never been married, and had relied on her sister for companionship until she'd passed away, a decade earlier. Was that what Daphne had to look forward to? A big black hole of loneliness?

Not that Violet had always been lonely—Daphne knew that before she'd become too infirmed, Violet had a group she played canasta with on a regular basis. She took daily walks through the neighborhood, waving at all the neighbors. And she'd take a taxi to attend concerts at the Kennedy Center, or visit the Smithsonian's National Portrait Gallery when she really got a wild hair. Over the years Daphne grew to love her like the mother she'd lost as a young woman. And she cared for her as she would have her own. She brought meals to her most days, and sat with her over coffee as they lamented the state of the world today and Violet reassured her that things were always bad on some level and not to fret about it too much. They'd watch movies or Netflix or play Scrabble (Violet always won) and it would be almost like a date, minus the making out and heavy petting. Heavy petting. Daphne rolled her eyes. She'd forgotten what that even was. Except when it came to her Labrador, Tortellini, who really was the love of her life and deserved all the pets she got.

She heaved a sigh and resolved to do something about the fact that she did nothing. Well, maybe tomorrow.

It wasn't a but a week or two after the memorial service that Daphne got the letter in the mail.

My dearest Daphne,

I hope you realize that you have been like a daughter to me for many years, and I have been forever grateful for your willingness to amuse this old gal and treat me like family. For all intents and purposes, you have been my only family, but for a second nephew twice removed or some such nonsense. I never could get those things right. Maybe he's a grand-nephew? One of those things. I was prepared to leave quite literally everything to you, however I made a promise long ago to my sister that I would include him in benefiting from the estate upon my death since he's lost his own parents too young. My largest asset is this duplex that you've been renting from me for the past however many years. I know you've worked hard to sock away money to eventually buy a place, but I'd like you to stop worrying about that. So I am leaving the entire contents of my life to you, and the actual home to both you and my grand-nephew, or whatever it is he is. I've hardly seen him for years, so I'm sure he will be happy to do whatever you'd like as far as the property is concerned. I'm really only including him to appease my beloved sister.

I have left instructions with my attorney to reach out to him and you and help you do what you need to so you no longer have to rent and can become a

Hard to Get Over

home owner finally. Always remember, I love you,
Daphne. You're the daughter I never had.
   Much love,
   Violet

Daphne gasped. Violet left the bulk of her estate to her? That was far too generous. How could she accept it? But with Violet gone, how could she not? She looked around her place. All these years it just felt like a place where she was parking her things, not a place to grow roots. But now she could own it outright, and it would be her real forever home. She couldn't believe her good fortune. It was starting to look like tomorrow was finally here: she could really get her act together and start living her best life.

Chapter Two

BRADY McGovern had been giving some real thought to settling down. Sometime soon. And why not now? He'd been wandering for a long time. Traveling, picking up odd jobs, traveling some more. Returning home to Seattle every now and then to see some friends, but never feeling a strong enough need to stay there. With his parents gone and no siblings, it just wasn't quite the same.

Frankly, the itinerant life wasn't abnormal to Brady. Having grown up in a military family, he never did feel particularly planted anywhere. One year here, two years there, he did get to experience living abroad, which was cool, but he also never got to experience continuity, which was tough as a kid. The longest time he stayed in one place was during college in North Carolina. Four years in Chapel Hill was great but more than enough time in one town. He'd taken off the day after graduation. His only regret was flaking out on a girl he'd recently started dating. Never even told her goodbye, just left. He needed the freedom of the open road, no ties holding him back. At first, he wandered around the States, camping and hiking in National parks. He even set about to hike the tallest mountain in each state. It took him two years, but he did it. Just in time to learn that his parents had died in a small plane crash. He never got a chance to say goodbye.

That hit him hard. After that he took off for parts

unknown. Bought a plane ticket to India and went on from there to several continents over the next several years. Sure, insurance money from his folks' estate gave him the luxury of wandering aimlessly. And for a while it helped him to seek out the rest of the world, to try to make sense of it all having gone sideways for him.

He was about to board a flight to London when he noticed on his phone that got an email from some attorney, which was weird, because it wasn't like he dealt with attorneys for anything.

He opened the email, and scanned it quickly before he boarded the plane and would lose his WiFi. His eyes scanned the words. Great Aunt Violet. Property in Washington, DC, area. She was leaving it to him and some woman who rented half of the place from her to divvy up however they saw fit. Huh. Weird. He vaguely remembered meeting her. Was she like his mother's aunt's sister or something like that? Hell, he had no idea. They were never around growing up to spend time with family.

He heard the gate person make an announcement for final boarding call and stuck his phone in his pocket. He'd deal with that later.

Two weeks later it was wheels-down at Washington Dulles airport. He was going to check out this windfall he hadn't expected. The attorney had sent him the key and the address and he was in an Uber on his way to the house now. He figured he'd spend a couple of days meeting with folks about selling the place, and get on the road as soon as it was all under control.

It was just settling on dark when he arrived at the house. A light drizzle was coming down as he exited the Uber. He stumbled on some broken piece of concrete on the walkway as he approached the house. He squinted. Huh. It was like two houses in one. One side was pitch black, the other had lights on. He turned on the light on his phone to avoid any more trip hazards and arrived at the door. He dropped his heavy backpack on the ground with a thud, and grabbed the key from his pocket, fumbling around to fit it into the deadbolt keyhole.

Just as he finally got the key in and the lock turning, a porch light behind him came on.

"Who are *you*?" he heard a stern, accusatory female voice behind him.

He jiggled the key out as he opened the door.

"Oh, hey, I'm Violet's, well, Violet was my, well, some sort of aunt," he said, reaching out his hand. "Brady. Brady McGovern. And you are?"

The woman stared at him, not extending her hand.

"You mean Brady-who-evaporated-into-thin-air-the-day-after-graduation-McGovern?"

He lifted a brow. Huh. That didn't sound good. He lifted his sunglasses up onto his head, not even noticing until then that he still had them on. No wonder it was so damned dark. And then he saw who was standing in front of him.

"Uh, Daphne?" he grimaced. What were the chances the woman he dumped as he checked his way out of the real world would be the person who he apparently had to figure out selling this place with? He smiled, and went in for a hug. "Hey! Daphne! Great to see you!"

She stood stock still, her arms tightly pressed to her sides.

Hard to Get Over

"Great to see you? Are you kidding me? I can't think of anyone I'd rather not see at this very minute. Or any other time, for that matter."

Brady scrubbed his hands across his face. "Look, Daph—"

"Don't 'Daph' me."

"Look, Daphne, it's late. I'm tired, I'm on Greenwich Mean Time or something like that. Looks like we've got some figuring out to do. What say we meet over coffee in the morning to come up with a game plan?"

She glared at him. "Yeah, right. Last time I had plans to meet with you the next day, I never saw you again."

He shook his head. Damn, looking at her, even angry, she was a sight for sore eyes. She was even hotter than she was in college. Tall, athletic build, gorgeous set of tits, tight little butt, from what he could tell with her standing kind of sideways to him. Despite being filled with fury at the moment, her blue eyes were still mesmerizing. And that black hair of hers, he was remembering now what it felt like as his fingers twined through her hair as she went down on him. Well, shit. Maybe that was the wrong thought because now he was feeling his cock swell in his pants. Not quite the greeting she was looking for, no doubt. Maybe it was a mistake for having ditched her like that.

"Can we talk about this later? I'm really beat. I need to get some shut-eye and then we can figure out about selling this thing. I'm thinking we can have it on the market in a couple of days. I did a little research, the market's super hot here right now, we'll be good to go."

She crossed her arms across her chest. He chest that he was struggling not to stare at. "Excuse me? On the market?"

"Well, yeah. We have to sell this thing. No point in keeping it."

She gave him one of those "are you a fucking moron" looks, her eyes squinted, her brow knit tight. "I beg to differ. This is my home, little runaway. You might not understand the value of home, but I certainly do, and this is where I am planting my roots."

Brady scratched at the two-day-old scruff on his face. He needed a bite to eat, a stiff drink and a bed, suddenly. He did not need some pissed-off ex flipping her shit on him precisely now.

"Okay, well. Huh. Yeah. Um. So. Well. I'm gonna go to bed now and we'll talk tomorrow." He grabbed his backpack and pushed it into the foyer. "Good night, Daph."

As he turned to go inside, he saw her stick her middle finger right up in his line of vision.

Well, crap. This wasn't going to be the cake walk he presumed it would be after all.

About Jenny

Jenny Gardiner is an award-winning #1 Kindle bestselling author who has published 37 novels, a memoir, and a collection of essays. Her work has been found in Ladies Home Journal, the Washington Post, Marie-Claire.com, Paste Magazine, and on National Public Radio. She is an occasional essayist on regional NPR affiliate WVTF-FM, and wrote a humorous column in Charlottesville's Daily Progress for over a decade as well as a food column for Cville Weekly Magazine. She has worked as a publicist for a United States senator, and as a freelance photographer, photographing such notable public figures as Prince Charles, Elizabeth Taylor, and the President of Uganda. She's been the volunteer coordinator for the Virginia Film Festival for ten years. She's really bad at math. Find her at www.jennygardiner.net